Martin Bridge
Out of Orbit!

Illustrated by
Joseph Kelly

Written by
Jessica Scott Kerrin

Kids Can Press

To Peter and Elliott, and to Joseph Kelly — the real
Spyder Mapleson. Also, special thanks to Joanne
and Michael, Florence and Tom, Kay and Steve, and
Paulette and Gene for shelter after the hurricane,
when these stories were written — J.S.K.

For Jessica Scott Kerrin, Debbie Rogosin and Julia Naimska.
Life gave us lemonade, and we made limoncello! — J.K.

Text © 2007 Jessica Scott Kerrin
Illustrations © 2007 Joseph Kelly

Kids Can Press acknowledges the financial support of the Government of Ontario,
through the Ontario Media Development Corporation's Ontario Book Initiative;
the Ontario Arts Council; the Canada Council for the Arts; and the Government
of Canada, through the BPIDP, for our publishing activity.

Published in Canada by
Kids Can Press Ltd.
29 Birch Avenue
Toronto, ON M4V 1E2

Published in the U.S. by
Kids Can Press Ltd.
2250 Military Road
Tonawanda, NY 14150

www.kidscanpress.com

Edited by Debbie Rogosin
Designed by Julia Naimska
Printed and bound in Canada

The art in this book was drawn
with graphite and charcoal;
shading was added digitally.

The text is set in GarthGraphic.

The hardcover edition of this book
is smyth sewn casebound.

The paperback edition of this book
is limp sewn with a drawn-on cover.

CM 07 0 9 8 7 6 5 4 3 2 1
CM PA 07 0 9 8 7 6 5 4 3 2 1

**Library and Archives Canada
Cataloguing in Publication**

Kerrin, Jessica Scott
   Martin Bridge out of orbit! / written
by Jessica Scott Kerrin; illustrated by
Joseph Kelly.

ISBN 978-1-55453-148-6 (bound)
ISBN 978-1-55453-149-3 (pbk)

I. Kelly, Joseph II. Title.

PS8621.E77M367 2007   jC813'.6
C2007-901121-7

Kids Can Press is a l☺r\\us™ Entertainment company

Contents

Crosswalk • 6

Spyder • 58

Draw Zip Rideout! • 108

Meet ...

Martin

Martin's mom

Martin's dad

Stuart

Harper

Alex

Mrs. Keenan

Mrs. Crammond

Zip Rideout

Laila

Spyder Mapleson

Crosswalk

That's strange, thought Martin as he jumped off the bus.

A group of teachers stood bunched together on the school steps. When Martin got closer, he could hear angry voices, one on top of the other.

"Just look at how fast the traffic is clipping along!"

"It's outrageous!"

"Drivers are completely ignoring the school zone signs!"

The crowd gasped as a car sailed toward Mr. Avalon, the crosswalk monitor. He jabbed his stop sign at the zooming car and waved his fist when the driver didn't even slow down.

Martin stood off to the side but close enough to listen in. It was a technique he often used around grown-ups.

"We need traffic lights," said Martin's homeroom teacher, Mrs. Keenan. "That will stop the speeders."

"It would," agreed Principal Moody. "And I've written countless letters to the city. But no one will listen."

"We'll just have to try a new tactic," Mrs. Keenan replied. She paused to watch Harper, one of Martin's classmates, get off his bike and cross with Mr. Avalon after a stream of motorcycles gunned by. "What about a parade?" she suggested.

A parade! Martin had never been in one before! He almost whooped, but then remembered to keep quiet.

"You might be on to something," said Principal Moody, stroking his gray beard. "Parades *are* hard to ignore."

The crowd buzzed in agreement. Martin nodded, too. Then the bell rang, and everyone bustled inside. Martin couldn't wait to tell his two best friends, Alex and Stuart.

"A parade!" they exclaimed. "Really?!"

"That's what I heard," said Martin with authority.

Several days later, Mrs. Keenan announced the details of the parade. It would happen first thing Monday morning.

Mr. Avalon would lead the march, and

everyone was encouraged to wear costumes.

Laila's hand shot up. As usual, her big curly hair blocked Martin's view of the blackboard.

"Can I dress up as a fairy princess?"

"You can go as anything you want," said Mrs. Keenan. "The more attention-grabbing, the better. We need to make the news."

Laila wheeled around to beam at Martin. She did that about a hundred times a day. It was annoying.

"Martin," said Mrs. Keenan, "perhaps you could wear your lobster outfit."

Martin's mom had made it for last year's school play. *Everyone* loved that costume.

"Sure thing," said Martin.

And for the rest of the morning, he had happy thoughts about wearing his lobster suit again.

Lunch talk orbited around costume
ideas for the parade. Even Alex and Stuart
wanted to come up with something new.
They had been underwater boulders in
last year's play and did not want a repeat
performance.

The boys were deep in conversation
when Harper sat down beside them. Martin
stifled a groan.

Harper drove Martin crazy. He was always telling impossible stories. And whenever Martin challenged him on the details, Harper would say, "You'll see."

"*My* costume is going to be out of this world," boasted Harper.

Martin rolled his eyes. "Sure, Harper. What are *you* going to be?"

"You'll see," said Harper, and he turned away.

"What could be out of this world?" asked Alex curiously.

"He's exaggerating," said Martin. "Again."

Alex and Stuart looked perplexed.

"It's just like his bike," said Martin. "Remember?"

Martin could not forget. Last month, Harper had gone on and on about how he

was
getting a
new bike that
could actually fly. But
when he finally rode it to school,
his bike looked just like everyone else's.

"I thought you said your bike could fly,"
Martin had called out.

"My dad took off the jet packs," Harper
had explained, "until I get a little older."

The crowd had murmured in admiration.

Martin remained highly skeptical. "Old enough for jet packs yet?" he taunted whenever he spotted Harper on his bike.

"Not yet," Harper always replied without missing a beat. "But soon. You'll see."

It was infuriating.

And now, listening to Harper brag about his costume made Martin lose his appetite. He set down his sandwich.

"Hey, Stuart," he said under his breath. "Alex might believe Harper's out-of-this-world malarkey. But you know he's a phony, right?"

"You never can tell," said Stuart between bites of his apple.

Martin stared at Stuart in disbelief. Surely he was joking. Martin was about to  say so when Harper turned back to the group.

"Hey," he said, switching topics, "I almost got hit in the crosswalk once."

"Really?" asked Alex and Stuart together. They were all ears.

Not Martin. He drank his milk noisily and kept sucking on the straw long after the carton was empty.

Harper waited patiently for Martin to stop.

"Yes, and I had to leap out of the way," he continued when Martin finally put down the carton. "I jumped so high, the car passed right underneath me."

"There!" Martin blurted out. "Did you hear that?! It's ridiculous!"

"Really?" Alex said to Harper, ignoring Martin. "How'd you jump so high?"

"My mega malted energy shake," said Harper, oblivious to Martin's outburst. "I drink one every morning."

"Mega malted energy shake," Alex repeated carefully. "How do you make it?"

Martin watched in horror as Stuart scrambled for a pencil and paper. Was he really going to write down Harper's made-up recipe? Cripes!

Just then, the bell rang, and Martin was thankful to escape.

Martin was glad Harper was not his friend. He couldn't stand listening to Harper's outlandish claims. And he couldn't figure out why others didn't seem to mind.

Martin tossed his carton into the garbage, thinking he'd like to chuck Harper's stories in there as well.

On Friday, Mrs. Keenan went over the final details for the parade. Everyone was on board, including the school's bus drivers, who were going to decorate their buses and flash their lights as they followed the marchers.

Laila's hand shot up.

"I have an extra costume at home," she said. "Maybe

others do, too. If we bring them in, more kids can dress up."

"Great idea, Laila!" said Mrs. Keenan.

Laila wheeled around, but this time she beamed at Harper in the next row over.

It was then Martin realized that no one was talking about his lobster costume anymore. Instead, more and more classmates had joined in the speculation about what Harper would wear.

Unbelievable!

Martin fumed.

Later that morning, Mrs. Crammond, their art teacher, launched into her lesson.

"I've put up the paintings of your houses that you did last week. Let's have a look at them, shall we?"

The first thing Martin noticed was that all the houses looked alike. Each one had a door with windows on either side, a smoking chimney and a picket fence. Some had a tree or a blazing sun or a bird flying by. Pretty ordinary stuff.

Then he happily observed that *his* painting was a cut above the rest. It featured his mom's flower boxes, his dad's lawn mower in the driveway and Martin's bedroom window with rocket-covered curtains.

"Wonderfully realistic details," observed Mrs. Crammond as the class gathered in front of Martin's painting.

Martin shrugged modestly. He was used to compliments about his artwork.

But then something in the display case caught his eye.

"What's that?" he asked. He knew Mrs. Crammond reserved the case for the very best art.

"That's *my* house," announced Harper proudly.

Harper's painting featured turrets, a drawbridge and a moat.

"You don't live in a castle," said Martin with a level glare.

"Well now, Martin," said Mrs. Crammond, an amused look on her face. "Harper's just being imaginative. Aren't you?" She smiled at Harper.

Harper beamed.

Cripes! "Harper doesn't live in a castle," insisted Martin. "I've ridden my bike past his house a million times. It's just a house!"

But despite Martin's protests, the class continued to admire Harper's work.

At lunch, Harper sat near Martin and his friends once again. Even though Harper's back was to them, Martin could see that he was tilting his head slightly, listening in on their conversation. It was a technique Martin was familiar with.

Martin was about to suggest they move, when Stuart spoke.

"Guess what?" he said. "My dad ordered the wood for my tree fort. We're going to start building it this weekend!"

"What's your tree fort going to have?" asked Harper, worming his way into the conversation.

"A trapdoor, a rope ladder and a sign that says 'Keep Out,'" listed Stuart as he counted off on his fingers. "Just like Martin's."

Martin smiled at Stuart's compliment.

"What about secret spy things?" asked Harper. "Like cameras and motion detectors. Does Martin's tree fort have those?"

"You bet," said Martin dryly, anger flaring. "And laser guns and a pool of sharks swimming around the base of the tree." He clucked his tongue. It was just like Harper to suggest that Martin's tree fort wasn't all that special.

"My dad can get those for you, Stuart," said Harper, ignoring Martin. "Cameras and motion detectors, I mean." Then he lowered his voice and darted his eyes left and right. "That's because he's a spy."

"What?!" demanded Martin. He squeezed his carton so hard, it burped milk all over his hand.

"Your dad's a spy?" repeated Stuart. He and Alex looked at Harper in awe.

Harper nodded.

"Your dad's *not* a spy!" Martin exclaimed. He grabbed some napkins to soak up the mess.

"He is too," said Harper with absolute conviction. He didn't even blink.

"I happen to know your dad owns a hardware store!" Martin

argued. "Whenever we buy paint, he's at the counter. And he wears one of those paint smock things and a name badge."

"That's his disguise," explained Harper. He winked at Alex and Stuart.

"Wow!" they said in hushed admiration.

"He's *not* a spy!" yelled Martin. "And you *don't* live in a castle. And your bike's *never* going to get off the ground!" Martin snatched up his lunch and stormed out.

At recess, when Mrs. Crammond stopped Martin in the hall to ask if he would paint the parade banner, the black cloud over his head moved off for a bit.

But by the end of the day, Martin had a full-blown thunderstorm raging in his head. Lightning struck when he spotted Harper blabbing with Alex and Stuart on the school steps. Martin could make out snippets of their conversation as he huffed by.

"Is your costume *really* going to be out of this world?" asked Stuart eagerly.

"I bet it will be a blast!" said Alex.

Harper grinned and rocked on his heels.

Martin couldn't help it. He stopped in his tracks and whirled around.

"Enough already!" he yelled. "Your

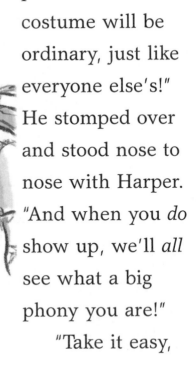

costume will be ordinary, just like everyone else's!" He stomped over and stood nose to nose with Harper. "And when you *do* show up, we'll *all* see what a big phony you are!"

"Take it easy,

Martin!" said Alex, putting his arm around
Harper's shoulders.

Stuart also took a supportive step
toward Harper, but he was stopped by
Martin's hostile glare.

"Harper makes things up!" Martin
shouted. "Why can't you all see that?!" He
wheeled back to Harper. "I suppose you'll
be wearing jet packs? Just like your bike?!"

"You'll see," said Harper calmly.

Martin felt as if his head would explode.

That night,
Martin lay awake
loathing Harper.
Even worse, he was
certain that Harper
was fast asleep, not
a worry in his head.

Martin angrily
punch-fluffed his
pillow. How could
Harper do it? Make such wild claims?

Unless ...

Martin sat bolt upright.

Could there be any truth in Harper's
words this time? Could he really have an
out-of-this-world costume that would make
Martin's lobster suit look like yesterday's
catch?

Martin's head began to spin. It *couldn't* be true. But just in case, Martin needed a costume even more spectacular than whatever Harper had dreamed up.

He flopped back down on his bed.

But what?

Staring across the dimly lit room, he could barely make out his rocket collection.

Then it came to him like a shooting star.

"Can I be an astronaut for the parade?" he asked his mom as soon as she came down to breakfast Saturday morning. "Like Zip Rideout?"

Zip Rideout, Space Cadet, was Martin's favorite cartoon hero.

"What about your lobster outfit?" she asked.

"We're supposed to bring in extra costumes so everyone has one," he said, for once grateful to Laila. His mom took a sip of coffee as she considered his request.

Martin held his breath.

"When's the parade, again?" she finally asked.

"Monday."

Martin's mom sighed in a way that told Martin he had won.

Together, they bought silvery space-age fabric

and badges and
flashing lights. For
two days, Martin
heard the whir of
the sewing machine.
It took his mom all

weekend to build the new costume — a
space suit, a helmet, and even a rocket
booster that he could strap to his back!

"Onwards and
upwards," said
Martin proudly
while she adjusted
his shoulder pads.
It was something
Zip Rideout said
at the start of
every mission.

"You look out of this world!" said Martin's dad, coming into the room for a look.

Mission accomplished, Martin thought with a satisfied smile.

On Monday morning, Martin scrambled out of bed. After donning his space gear, he dug out the lobster costume from his closet. But with his knapsack and lunchbox, it was too much to carry.

"I can drive you," offered his dad.

Martin gratefully tossed him the keys.

"There's my banner!" said Martin as they pulled up to the front of the school.

Mrs. Crammond had taped it across one side of the steps from railing to railing.

"Well done, Sport," said Martin's dad.

Martin got out and waved good-bye. He lumbered up the other side of the steps

with his gear. He was about to step inside when the sound of another vehicle made him turn around.

It was Harper's dad. No one could miss his van. It had enormous hardware store logos plastered on its sides.

Some disguise, thought Martin.

Then he realized that if he waited, Harper would be the first to see Martin's *truly* out-of-this-world costume. And surely that would put an end to Harper's ludicrous fabrications once and for all.

Martin set down his cumbersome things just inside the door, then confidently stepped back out and stood at the top of the stairs. His astronaut suit sparkled in the sun.

The van door flew open. Martin smiled

radiantly as Harper climbed out. One silver leg, then two, then a rocket booster and finally, a helmet.

Martin gasped and quickly ducked behind his banner.

Harper was an astronaut.

Just like Martin.

"Wait, Dad!" called Harper before the van door slid shut.

He reached in and pulled out a light saber.

Harper was an astronaut with a light saber. He turned it on. A light saber with batteries! He bounded up the steps and into the school.

Martin stood up slowly.

"No fair!" he shouted.

Furious, Martin whirled around to go inside. But his rocket booster got caught on the banner, and the banner ripped in two.

Martin staggered backward, devastated. His world was spinning out of orbit.

"Hey!" called a fairy princess who had just rounded the corner of the school and was flouncing toward him. "Why'd you do that?"

Martin didn't have time to explain. He decided it would be far better to wear his old costume than to go as a lesser version of Harper. So he bolted inside, scooped up

his belongings and dashed to the boys'
locker room.

Sadly, Martin took off his rocket

booster and
climbed out of
his space suit.
It puddled at
his feet, a
flattened pool
of shimmering
gray. Then he
reluctantly put
on the lobster
costume. As
he did, he
accidentally
kicked his
helmet across

the floor. It rolled away, hit the wall and bounced back toward him.

Martin stared at the helmet as it landed at his feet. He reached for it.

A-ha!

Instead of the lobster head, he put the helmet back on and looked in the mirror. He needed one more thing. A rocket booster! He strapped it into place and saluted himself.

Perfect!

Martin was no longer an *ordinary* astronaut like Harper. Now he was an astronaut *from Mars*! A slow smile crept across his face.

The bell rang as Martin paraded into the classroom.

"Holy cow!" said Alex appreciatively.

"Terrific Martian costume!" agreed Stuart.

Martin saluted them with a giant red claw. Smugly, he took his seat, then turned to gloat at Harper. But Harper's seat was empty.

"Where's Harper?" asked Martin.

"Principal's office," whispered Stuart.

"What'd he do?" Martin whispered back.

"Ripped your banner in half," Alex said in a hushed tone.

"What?!" exclaimed Martin.

"Laila caught him red-handed," said Stuart.

The fairy princess in front of Martin wheeled around in her seat and grinned at him.

Martin slid his giant red claws under the desk. He realized with awful certainty that Laila had seen *him* rip the banner, not Harper. Cripes.

"When we asked Harper why he did it,"

continued Alex, "he said he didn't know what we were talking about."

"But we didn't believe him," said Stuart. "You know how he makes things up. You were right about Harper all along."

Martin said nothing.

"Attention, class!" called Mrs. Keenan, stepping smartly into the room with her clipboard.

Martin struggled to focus on her instructions about the parade, but his ears were on fire.

She was almost done when there was a sharp knock at the door. Mrs. Keenan stepped outside, then motioned for Martin to join her. He got up nervously.

Mrs. Hurtle, the school secretary, stood in the hall. She turned to Martin and said gravely, "Principal Moody wants to see you."

"Why?" he squeaked, his stomach flip-flopping madly.

She lowered her voice. "I think he wants to give Harper the chance to apologize."

Martin's heart began to pound. He marched stiffly down the long empty hallway, Mrs. Hurtle clickety-clacking beside him. Harper sat waiting on the wooden bench just outside the principal's door.

Martin's pangs of guilt quickly dissolved. Seeing Harper as an astronaut with the added bonus of a light saber made Martin mad all over again.

"Shove over," he said gruffly.

"I didn't touch your banner," said Harper glumly.

"Well, that's not what everyone thinks,"

said Martin, staring straight ahead.

The telephone rang, and Mrs. Hurtle picked up the receiver. From the way she was answering questions, Martin could tell she was talking to a reporter.

"No one will believe me," said Harper pitifully. His shoulders sagged.

"Why would they?" demanded Martin.

"You exaggerate all the time."

They sat in silence for a while, Harper mulling this over.

But Martin had something to mull over, too. And it was making his hands sweat under the claws.

"Martin?" Harper finally said in a small voice as he took off his helmet.

"What?" Martin replied coldly. He readied himself for Harper's next impossible story.

"My dad isn't really a spy."

Astounded, Martin turned to Harper.

"No kidding," he said, eyebrow raised.

"Sometimes I say things ... well, you know, for attention." Harper scuffed at the floor. "I know my turrets and jet packs aren't real like your rocket-covered curtains or your tree fort with its 'Keep Out' sign."

He shrugged and gave Martin a quick, apologetic smile.

Martin was silent. Somehow, Harper's confession had softened Martin's anger.

So what if Harper embellished? At least his stories didn't hurt anybody. And besides, Martin had to admit that it was kind of fun to think about a bike with jet packs, even if it *was* a long shot.

Martin pulled off his helmet, too.

"I know you didn't ruin my banner. I did," he admitted. "Accidentally," he added.

"Are you going to tell?" asked Harper.

"Yes," said Martin with relief.

More silence, and then Harper turned on his light saber. It blinked.

"I don't suppose astronauts carry light sabers," said Harper sheepishly, "but Martians might. Do you want to borrow mine?"

Gingerly, he held out the saber to Martin.

Martin didn't hesitate. "Sure!" he

said, mesmerized by all the flashing lights.

Outside, the school was gathering for the parade. From the window, they could see Mr. Avalon taping the banner back together. Brightly costumed students were milling about on the sidewalk. And decorated school buses were slowly moving into position.

55

Mrs. Hurtle put her hand over the receiver. "I have a reporter here who wants to interview a student about the crosswalk." She held the telephone toward them. "Does one of you want to speak to her?" Martin thought quickly. He knew the school badly needed traffic lights. He knew how important it was to get reporters out to the parade. And he knew he was sitting beside someone with enough imagination to get them to come.

"You do it, Harper," said Martin as he turned off the saber and settled back on the bench.

He was ready for a good Harper story.

Spyder

One by one, Martin's classmates announced what they wanted to be when they grew up.

Martin could think of nothing more exciting than exploring bold, uncharted worlds like his cartoon hero, Zip Rideout, Space Cadet. So when his turn came, he proudly replied, "Astronaut."

Just like his two best friends, Alex and Stuart.

It turned out that astronaut was the most popular answer in Martin's class, with a few firefighters, police officers, hockey players, paleontologists and ballerinas sprinkled in.

"I'm delighted there are so many astronauts in the room," said their art teacher, Mrs. Crammond, "because I have a special surprise for you."

She paused so that the class could buzz with speculation. When everyone was fit to spin out of orbit, she announced, "I've arranged for an illustrator to visit our school. And this illustrator *loves* astronauts."

Martin's stomach did a happy little leap. He knew what illustrators did. They drew for posters and magazines and stuff.

And the work of his favorite illustrator was right there in his desk. Martin reached in and pulled out a dog-eared comic book.

The cover featured Zip Rideout moonwalking across a steamy crater, his rocket standing at attention in the distance.

The story was written and illustrated by Spyder Mapleson. It said so right beneath Zip's rocket.

"I'll give you a hint about who it is," said Mrs. Crammond. She walked over to Martin's desk and held up his comic book.

"Spyder Mapleson?!" gasped Martin.

"That's right!" said Mrs. Crammond, handing back the comic book.

The class whooped while Martin happily clutched Zip's picture to his chest.

Mrs. Crammond returned to the front of the studio.

"He's coming Monday, and we need

to get this room shipshape for his visit."

"*Space* shipshape," Martin called out, all smiles.

"Very good, Martin," Mrs. Crammond said. "So today we'll paint scenes from outer space to decorate the studio."

They quickly set up their easels, and Martin jumped right to work with his brush. Art was his favorite class, and space exploration was his favorite subject.

He decided he would paint Zip Rideout giving his official salute. But when it came time to add Zip's badge of honor, Martin had trouble with the silver points.

I'll have to ask Spyder Mapleson how to paint realistic details, thought Martin, and I'll take really good notes so that I remember every word.

When the class was almost over, Mrs. Crammond clapped her hands. "Time to put your work up," she announced.

The students pinned their art to the walls of the studio, transforming the classroom into a space academy. Martin was pleased to see that he was the only one who had tackled Zip's portrait.

The other astronauts had painted
satellites and planets with many moons.

The firefighters had featured flaming
rockets and exploding suns.

The police officers had drawn
intergalactic battle scenes.

The hockey players had designed
protective space gear.

And the paleontologists and ballerinas

had created futuristic museums and theaters filled with patrons who looked surprisingly like dinosaurs.

"Mrs. Crammond?" said Martin after surveying the room. "I think we should write Zip Rideout's loyalty pledge on the blackboard."

The class murmured their approval.

"How does it go?" she asked, picking up a piece of chalk.

The class recited the pledge while Mrs. Crammond wrote it out in her tidy teacher's handwriting.

From star to star my ship will race,
The speed of light is my fast pace,
It's bold, uncharted worlds I'll face
'Cause I'm a brave cadet of space.

Then everyone gave each other the official Zip Rideout salute.

That Saturday, Martin sat in the cool shade of his tree fort with Alex and Stuart. They had their Solar System Explorer Sets and were deciding which *Zip Rideout* show to act out.

"How about episode twenty-six: 'Return of Crater Man'?" suggested Stuart.

Martin knew all about episode twenty-six. Zip fought off Crater Man in a shoot-out on the planet Astro. It had been scary to watch because Martin was sure Zip would get hurt.

But Zip didn't. As usual, he was able to
dart away from the blasts and still manage
to capture his archenemy in an ingenious
trap.

"Sounds good to me!" exclaimed Martin
and Alex together.

The three put on their official Zip Rideout
space goggles.

"I'll be Ground
Control," said
Stuart. "Where are
the walkie-talkies?"

Martin dug
them out from
under the old
ship's wheel that
his dad had bought
at a yard sale. He

handed one of the walkie-talkies to Stuart.

"I'll be Zip," said Martin.

He knew Alex wouldn't mind. Alex had been Zip the last time.

"Then I'll be the King of Astro," said Alex, agreeably enough. "And I'll help Zip free my people from Crater Man's evil grip."

"Okay," said Martin. "Let's take our places."

Stuart climbed down the ladder to set up Ground Control at the base of the tree, while Zip and the King of Astro stayed up top and discussed their lines.

"Testing, testing. One, two, three. Testing," squawked Martin's walkie-talkie.

"Ground Control,

this is Zip. Over," said Martin in his official radio voice.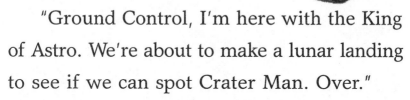

"I read you, Zip. Over."

"Ground Control, I'm here with the King of Astro. We're about to make a lunar landing to see if we can spot Crater Man. Over."

"Affirmative, Zip. This is Ground Control standing by. Radio again when you've touched down."

"Roger," said Martin, very Zip-like.

Martin quickly replayed the next scene in his head. Moonwalking was going to be a blast. No wonder he wanted to be an astronaut when he grew up!

"You know what would be fun?" Alex asked in his regular voice. "If we could *really* feel what it would be like to moonwalk."

Martin nodded and looked out the window of his tree fort. "Well, we're high enough. We just need the bounce part."

"Say, I have an idea. Where's your pogo stick?" asked Alex.

"The garage," said Martin, instantly on high alert. "Why?"

Alex was always full of harebrained ideas, like rescuing Polly, their class parakeet, from another school, bringing slime to Camp Kitchywahoo as a prank and locking his brother out of their bedroom by gluing the door shut.

"You'll see," said Alex, and he grabbed Martin's walkie-talkie. "Ground Control? This is the King of Astro. Do you read me? Over."

"I read you loud and clear. Over."

"Astro's orange moon has just come up on our sensors. We're going to need our antigravity bounce device. Over."

"Say again. Over."

"Our antigravity bounce device. Over."

There was a long pause, and dead air filled both walkie-talkies.

At last, Martin took pity on Stuart. He grabbed the walkie-talkie from Alex.

"My pogo stick, Stuart. It's in the garage," explained Martin.

"Roger," said Ground Control. Then, forgetting to turn off his walkie-talkie, Stuart muttered, "Why didn't they just say so?"

Alex rolled his eyes at Martin. Martin adjusted his space goggles.

A few minutes later, Stuart pushed open the trapdoor.

"We should switch roles soon," he said peevishly. "I'm getting bored down there."

"In a bit," said Alex,

taking the pogo stick from him.

Reluctantly, Stuart headed down to his post, banging the trapdoor shut behind him.

"Watch this," said Alex eagerly.

He jumped on the pogo stick and began to bounce erratically around the tree fort.

"Stay clear of the window," advised Martin. "It's a long way down." Something in his own voice reminded Martin of the worried tone his mom sometimes had.

"This is great," announced Alex, ignoring Martin's warning. He smoothed out his bounce. "I'm ... practically ... floating ... in ... space," he said between sproings.

It began to look like a lot of fun, and the cautious voice inside Martin's head faded away.

"Let me try," said Martin.

Alex bounced a few more times before surrendering the pogo stick.

During his first few tries, Martin kept falling off to avoid hitting a wall or getting too close to the window. It was dizzying being so high up and in such a tight space. He decided to take smaller bounces to get better control.

"Look at me!" exclaimed Martin.

Bounce. Bounce.

"I'm moonwalking! Just like Zip on my comic book cover!"

It was then that Stuart, a look of curiosity on his face,
pushed the trapdoor wide open.

"What's going on?" he demanded. But he barely finished his question because,

at that exact moment, Martin bounced past Stuart and rocketed through the open trapdoor.

Later, Alex and Stuart would say it all happened so quickly.

But not Martin.

As he plunged down, Martin saw everything in exquisite detail. Stuart, whose mouth was shaped like the capital letter O. The tree fort ladder flickering by like a picket fence. A squirrel staring quizzically and chattering at him to slow down. And the lawn springing up to meet him.

Then the pogo stick landed. It stayed put, but Martin kept going. He launched back into the air, passing that same chattering squirrel, then smashed high up against the tree.

Martin slid down the rough bark until he came to rest in a soft puddle position at the base of the trunk.

Alex and Stuart scrambled down the ladder.

"Martin! Martin! Are you okay?" they called.

Martin didn't move. He sat, woozy and confused.

"Get up! Get up!" Alex ordered. "My dad always makes me do that right away to make sure nothing's broken."

But Martin did not get up. His ears

were ringing, and even though Alex was
talking right to Martin's face, his words
sounded far, far away. Martin peeled off
his Zip Rideout goggles.

"He's bleeding," said Stuart, wringing
his hands and stepping back behind Alex.

"Where?" asked Alex.

Stuart pointed to the side of Martin's
head precisely where Martin felt burning.

It also throbbed every time his heart beat.

"Holy cow!" said Alex.

Martin reached up and gingerly touched the side of his head. It felt warm and sticky. He looked at his fingertips.

Blood.

The ground flew up to grab him, but Alex lunged forward to hold Martin steady against the tree trunk.

"H-how bad is it?" Martin asked
tentatively, not sure if he really wanted
to know. He half-turned his head so his
friends could take a better look.

Alex and Stuart leaned in to investigate,
then Stuart quickly pulled back.

"What?!" Martin demanded, alarmed by
Stuart's reaction.

His friends glanced at each other with
big eyes. It was Stuart who finally spoke.

"You're bleeding behind the flappity
part of your ear," he reported.

"The what?" Martin asked weakly. The
ground wobbled again.

"Behind your ear flap," Alex confirmed.
"Someone should look at that."

Stuart nodded vigorously.

Now the side of Martin's head throbbed

even more. Everything became swirly again. Martin started to shake.

"I'll go get your mom," offered Stuart, and he dashed across the lawn before Martin could protest.

Alex stayed with Martin. There followed a brief but tense silence.

"Holy cow! You should have seen yourself," Alex finally blurted out. "One minute you're moonwalking, and the next minute — *whoosh* — you've gone through a wormhole in space!"

Martin said nothing. It took great effort not to throw up.

"And look at this," said Alex, scrambling to his feet and scooting over to where the pogo stick had speared the ground. It was still standing at a rakish angle.

"I can't even pull this out," he said, yanking it dramatically with both hands. He looked to Martin for approval but was interrupted by a shout.

"Martin!"

Martin looked up at the sound of his mom's voice as she sprinted across the yard, then hunkered down in front of him.

"Let me see," she said softly, turning Martin's head so that the mashed side faced her.

"Oh, my." She gently prodded his pounding ear flap. "You boys wait with Martin. I'll get the first aid kit."

In a flash, she was gone. Alex turned to Stuart and started up again.

"Did you see Martin shoot through the trapdoor? It was like he rocketed through a wormhole. Like episode seven, when Zip travels from the desert planet of Bleeker to one of Astro's moons." He wheeled to face Martin. "No kidding, Martin. You were moving at the speed of light! Just like Zip Rideout!!"

Martin had always wanted to be just like his space hero, so Alex's words should have thrilled him. But they didn't.

Instead, Martin tried to remember an episode where Spyder Mapleson showed Zip in a lot of pain. Real pain. With blood. None came to mind. Not even the shoot-out scene with Crater Man. It was then that Martin realized he had been deceived.

"I don't want to be an astronaut anymore," Martin announced, Spyder Mapleson's betrayal exploding inside him.

His friends gasped.

"That's crazy," said Alex.

"Crazy?" repeated Martin. "No. Crazy is bouncing around on a pogo stick in a tree fort."

Alex scuffed at the ground.

"What about exploring bold, uncharted worlds?" asked Stuart.

"What do *you* know about exploring bold, uncharted worlds?" snapped Martin. "*You* chose Ground Control."

"Hang on!" Stuart replied in a hurt voice. "I said I was bored and wanted to switch. Remember?"

"Want to switch with me now?" asked Martin. He turned the throbbing side of his head to Stuart for full effect.

To Martin's satisfaction, Stuart quickly looked away.

Suddenly, Martin's mom was gently pressing a cool cloth to his head. But Martin couldn't remember how she got there. And he didn't remember getting into the van or how Alex and Stuart came to be riding in the backseat.

"Almost there," said Martin's mom.

"Almost where?" asked Martin.

"The hospital," said his mom, glancing at him.

The hospital? Cripes! Martin had never been to one before. But from what he had heard from Alex, who had been there plenty of times, it didn't sound like much fun.

"Why can't I just lie down in my room for a bit?" he asked feebly.

"This is an emergency, Martin," said his mom. She glanced at him again, this time with alarm. "I already explained this when we were helping you into the van."

Martin gave her a blank stare.

"We're *definitely* going to the hospital," she muttered, pushing harder on the gas pedal.

Looking back, Martin remembered bits and pieces about the hospital. Squeaky linoleum floors and voices calling over loudspeakers. Ceiling lights so bright there were no shadows in the room. And  being wheeled around on a hard cot with a pillow that made crinkle sounds beneath his head.

Alex and Stuart had to wait in the lobby while Martin got stitches behind his ear, but Martin's mom never left his side.

The next
thing Martin
knew, his
mom was
tucking him
in on the sofa
at home. She
had even
brought down
Admiral, Martin's furry stuffed turtle, and
the rocket-covered blanket from his bed.

"Want to watch some television?" she
asked kindly. "I think Zip's on."

This did not buoy Martin's spirits. He
was still angry at Spyder Mapleson because
of Zip's accident-free record.

Martin shook his head "no," but the
movement caused him sudden jabbing

pains. He winced, and his mom nodded sympathetically. She got him some apple juice and a pill for the pain.

"You'll be shipshape in no time," she assured him as he swallowed it.

Martin wasn't so certain. For as long as he could remember, Martin had believed in Zip. And every night he had dreamed of exploring bold, uncharted worlds. Now he knew better.

"Bought you a comic book, Sport," said Martin's dad later that day. "The newest *Zip Rideout!*"

"Thanks, Dad," Martin managed as he stared at yet another annoyingly triumphant cover.

Moonwalking. Rescue missions. *Shootouts!* Why, an astronaut was *bound* to get hurt. But as Martin flipped through the pages, he reaffirmed that there were no accidents or hospital scenes or blood in any of Spyder Mapleson's stories.

All lies, thought Martin bitterly.

He tossed the comic book down in disgust, then rolled over onto his non-mashed side. Moving his head still hurt.

"Ow! Ow! Ow!" he complained, Zip's

infuriating front-cover smile mocking him from the floor.

On Sunday, Martin mostly slept, but by Monday morning he was up and about.

"Are you sure you feel well enough to go to school, Sport?" asked his dad at breakfast. "The doctor said you could stay home for another day."

"Spyder Mapleson's coming for a visit," explained Martin's mom as she buttered some toast. "Martin wouldn't miss him for the world."

Martin said nothing. He poured his usual bowl of Zip Rideout Space Flakes, but he turned the box so he wouldn't have to look at the illustration of Zip's rocket.

It was then that Martin remembered he had wanted to ask Spyder Mapleson about how to paint realistic details.

Forget that, thought Martin. *Nothing* about Spyder Mapleson's illustrations was real. With angry determination, he began to develop a new line of questioning.

When Martin arrived at school, his bandages caused quite a sensation, and he had to explain the accident about a hundred times.

Alex kept trying to insert space hero details like moonwalking and wormholes into Martin's version of the event, but Martin wouldn't have any of it.

"I'm not like Zip," he insisted, head still slightly throbbing. "And I don't want to be."

He repeated this until art class, when he spotted Spyder Mapleson sitting beside Mrs. Crammond's desk. A box near the illustrator's feet had part of the solar system sticking out of it.

"Good morning," said Mrs. Crammond warmly after all of Martin's classmates had settled down. "As you know, we have a very special visitor today. Please welcome Spyder Mapleson."

The class clapped vigorously as their guest stood. He had very bushy eyebrows

and wore a black Zip Rideout T-shirt. He
gave them the official Zip Rideout salute.

Everyone jumped up and saluted back.
Martin grudgingly joined in. Then he

noticed that one of the planets orbiting out of Spyder Mapleson's box was Pluto.

That's not even a planet anymore, thought Martin in disgust as he sat back down.

Spyder Mapleson launched into his presentation. He talked about his artwork and where he got his ideas from. As he did, he pulled out the old-fashioned solar system and other space props from his box. Then he taped a large sheet of paper to the wall and showed them how to draw Zip Rideout step by step.

"And this is how I handle my ink brush to add details, like the star-shaped zipper pull and the badge of honor," explained Spyder, putting the finishing touches on Zip's jacket.

This was exactly the kind of information Martin had once hoped for.

"Aaaaaah!" said the class, much to Martin's annoyance.

Martin did not take notes.

"Any questions?" asked Spyder.

Hands shot up.

The astronauts were curious about why Astro's moon was orange. The firefighters were interested in Zip's most memorable explosion. The police officers wanted to find out if laser guns made sounds in space. The hockey players asked if  Zip's space suit protected him from flying debris. And the paleontologists and ballerinas wondered if Zip went to museums and theaters on his days off.

Martin rolled his eyes at all of Spyder Mapleson's answers.

"We have time for one more question," said Mrs. Crammond.

Martin raised his hand.

"My name is Martin, and I have a question," he said with the deadly aim of an intergalactic missile. "How come you never show pictures of accidents or blood or pain when Zip is exploring bold, uncharted worlds?"

"Good question, Martin," said Spyder.

"But before I answer, let me ask you this. Would you *want* to see pictures of accidents or blood or your space hero in pain?"

Martin didn't take long to answer. "No," he said as he touched his bandages.

The class murmured in agreement, glancing at Martin with sympathetic eyes.

"Precisely," said Spyder. "And that's one of the best things about being an illustrator. Sure, Zip gets to explore bold, uncharted worlds. But I get to *create* those worlds and Zip's space adventures. There's *nothing* more exciting than that!"

The class mulled this over.

Martin, too.

Like a misfired rocket booster, Martin's anger fizzled to nothing.

"Say, I have an idea for a world that

Zip could explore," said Martin.

"You do?" said Spyder. "Tell us."

"How about a planet where people live in tree forts?" suggested Martin.

"I like it," said Spyder, raising a bushy eyebrow in delight. He picked up his ink brush and began to sketch out the scene.

"And maybe they could get around on pogo sticks," Martin called out.

Spyder drew that, too.

"I think we should call them Martinians," said Spyder, adding the final details.

When he completed the drawing, he rolled it up and gave it to Martin along with the official Zip Rideout salute.

Martin saluted back.

Spyder Mapleson's visit ended, and Mrs. Crammond escorted him to the school's front door. Everyone quickly turned to Martin.

"Holy cow, Martin!" exclaimed Alex. "You think just like Spyder!"

"And I thought only astronauts got worlds named after them," added Stuart, fully impressed.

Martin beamed. He leapt up from his desk and raced over to his portrait of Zip, eager to add silver points, now that he knew how.

For although Martin hadn't taken any notes, he remembered every word.

Draw Zip Rideout!

Spyder Mapleson showed Martin's class how to draw their favorite superhero. Here are some tips to help you make Zip Rideout fly!

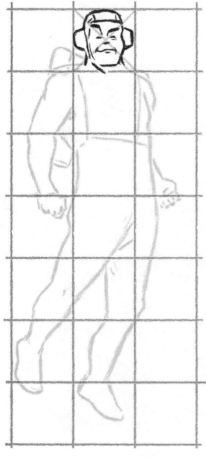

1. Draw a grid of squares, 3 squares wide and 7 high. Use graph paper to help you, or trace this grid.

2. Now you can draw Zip's face. Take your time, and put your lines in the top middle square, like this:

3. His flight helmet goes here.

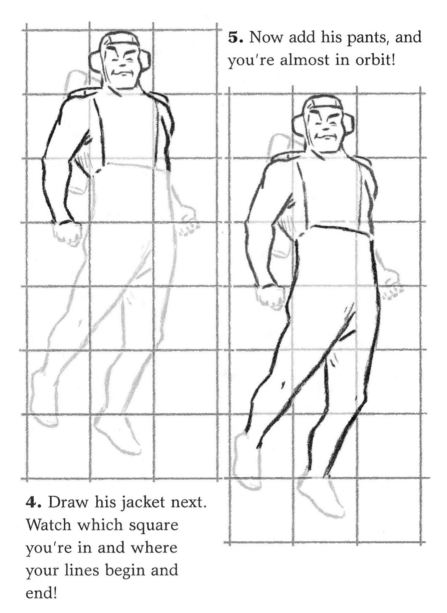

5. Now add his pants, and you're almost in orbit!

4. Draw his jacket next. Watch which square you're in and where your lines begin and end!

6. Now draw his hands, feet and rocket booster.

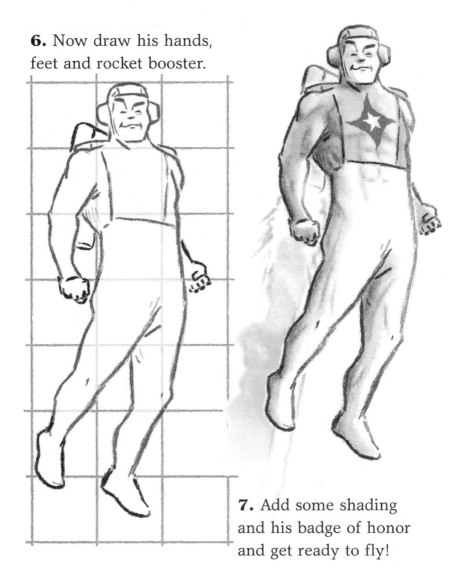

7. Add some shading and his badge of honor and get ready to fly!

Growing up, **Jessica Scott Kerrin** longed for a pogo stick or a tree fort or a bike that could actually fly. But unlike Zip Rideout, she did not have an accident-free record, and if she had gotten her wishes — ouch! — those things would have sent her completely out of orbit. She  did, however, get along well with board games. Jessica, a champion puzzle solver, lives with her family in Halifax, Nova Scotia.

 When **Joseph Kelly** was a boy, he drew spaceships, astronauts, robots, aliens and bold, uncharted worlds. Now, he gets to draw all that and more as he creates Martin's universe. Without a doubt this makes him the happiest man in Sonoma, California.

Catch up on all of Martin's adventures!

HC ISBN-13: 978-1-55337-688-0
PB ISBN-13: 978-1-55337-772-6

HC ISBN-13: 978-1-55337-689-7
PB ISBN-13: 978-1-55337-773-3

HC ISBN-13: 978-1-55337-961-4
PB ISBN-13: 978-1-55337-962-1

HC ISBN-13: 978-1-55337-976-8
PB ISBN-13: 978-1-55337-977-5

PB $4.95 US / $5.95 CDN • HC $14.95 US / $16.95 CDN

Written by Jessica Scott Kerrin • Illustrated by Joseph Kelly